The Dog-Next-Year

for Leah, who listened first and told me dreams
and for Andrea, bright new book-lover
—C.M.

to Bethany, for determination
Daniel, for laughter
Laurel, for vision
—N.K.

© 2001, Carmelita McGrath

Le Conseil des Arts | The Canada Council
du Canada | for the Arts

We acknowledge the support of The Canada Council for the Arts
for our publishing program.

We acknowledge the financial support of the Government of Canada through the
Book Publishing Industry Development Program (BPIDP)
for our publishing activities.

Illustrations © 2001, Nancy Keating

∞ Printed on acid-free paper

Published by TUCKAMOREBOOKS *an imprint of Creative Book Publishing*

A division of 10366 Newfoundland Limited A Robinson-Blackmore Associated Company

P.O. Box 8660, St. John's, Newfoundland A1B 3T7

Printed in Canada by: ROBINSON-BLACKMORE PRINTING & PUBLISHING

Canadian Cataloguing in Publication Data

McGrath, Carmelita

The dog-next-year

ISBN 1-894294-33-5

1. Dogs—Juvenile fiction.   I. Keating, Nancy   II. Title.

PS8575.G68D63   2001   jC813'.54   C2001-900433-8
P Z7.M16952Do   2001

The Dog-Next-Year

Carmelita McGrath

illustrated by
Nancy Keating

Tuckamore Books
a Creative Publishers imprint

St. John's, Newfoundland
2001

For the third evening in a row, Lissa came home from school and stared out the window, daydreaming. She looked at the garden growing dark already, and imagined a puppy standing between the maple and the dogberry tree. The small dog she imagined was wagging its tail, waiting for Lissa to come out and play.

Lissa almost asked her mother if she could go out in the garden and play with the dog, but she caught herself and said, "Can I go out and ride my bike before supper?"

"Bundle up," said her mother and Lissa did. She put on a sweater and a jacket and her purple scarf and her blue mittens with pompoms on them. She put on her hat with the long tail that streamed behind her like a kite. By the time she got on her bike, she could hardly move she had so much clothes on.

The backyard was small, so Lissa could not go as far or as fast as she wanted. She noticed that there were hardly any leaves left on the trees. She saw a clump of blue asters, a starling eating dog-berries and a ginger cat with a fat tail watching the starling. All the time she rode her bike, Lissa imagined a puppy running behind her, barking, scaring the cat and the starling, scattering the fallen leaves.

Lissa had a playhouse that you could walk into and pretend it was
your own house far away in the woods. She had a dollhouse with a
little switch that turned the lights off when it was time for the dolls
to go to sleep. She had a stegosaurus that flashed its eyes and
clacked its scales as it walked, scaring Abigail the cat. But what
Lissa wanted more than anything in the world was a dog.

"Pleeeeze," Lissa said at supper, "can I have a dog?"

"A dog is a BIG responsibility," said Lissa's father. And he made a long speech.

He talked about feeding, taking for walks, pooper-scoopers, vacations, vaccinations and a whole lot of other things that made Lissa stop listening.

"Sshh," said Lissa's mother finally, "I think Lissa understands. Having a dog is a BIG responsibility. But you're getting bigger, too, Lissa."

"I'm six." Lissa said.

"Exactly," said her mother. "Who knows — maybe you can get a dog next year."

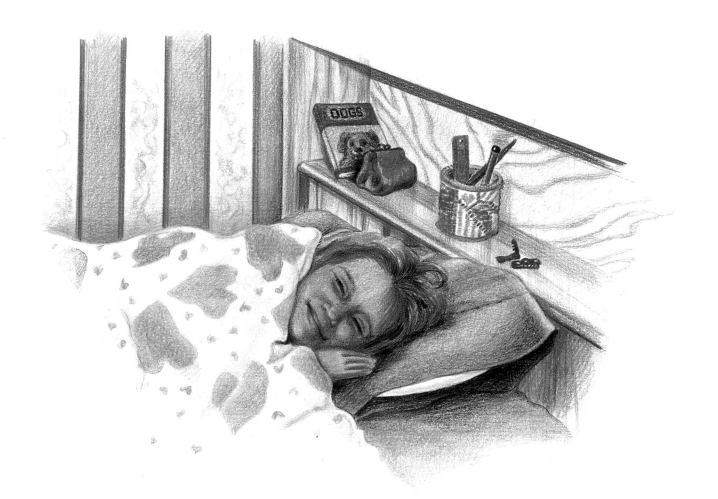

When Lissa was going to sleep, she thought about being seven and having a dog. Lissa imagined the Dog-Next-Year, and gave it a secret name. It would be a puppy. It would have brown and white fur that tickled her hands. The ears would be long and as soft as velvet. Lissa and the dog would run and tumble in the park, and in the summer they would go to the beach, and Lissa would throw pieces of driftwood and teach the dog to fetch. Going to sleep, Lissa called the dog by its secret name, and it came and ran with her through her dreams.

When Halloween came, Lissa went trick-or-treating with her friends Peter and Martha and all their parents. The sidewalks were wild with racing ghouls and shouting spirits. A scream ripped from a house next door. Lissa's mother jumped — and stepped in something a dog had left on the sidewalk.

"Yuk," said Lissa's mother. "You'd think people would clean up after their dogs!"

"Yuk," said Peter. "Dis-gus-ting!"

Lissa gave Peter a sharp nudge. She didn't want him agreeing with her mother about dogs and messes.

"If it was my dog, I'd clean up," Lissa said.

On Christmas morning when Lissa got up, she closed her eyes tight and thought for a minute about something small and silky and alive under the tree. She ran downstairs. Under the tree was a doll that could do gymnastics, a set of blocks for building cities in the living room, a modelling set for making monsters and four beautiful books. There were wrapped presents with secrets inside and a stocking that bulged, fat and crinkly with surprises. But no dog! *Next year...or my birthday*, Lissa thought.

She built an office tower out of blocks and pretended the doll was a giant. The doll tumbled into the tower, and blocks flew every-where.

"Look at me," Lissa's father said, and he took a picture of her smile.

Winter was gone before Lissa could notice it going. One day, there was a melting snowman all grey and brown on the sidewalk in front of Lissa's house and the next day there was only a pool of water.

Small purple and yellow flowers called crocuses appeared by Lissa's back steps. Then daffodil buds swelled and opened, and Lissa's garden was filled with a wonderful smell. It was time to go bike riding with Peter and Martha again. And it was almost time for Lissa's seventh birthday.

One night, close to her birthday, Lissa was so excited she couldn't sleep. At supper, Lissa and her parents had been planning the birthday party. Now, Lissa's parents were downstairs listening to music and playing Scrabble. That's what they always did on Friday night. Lissa could hear them talking. She could pick out their words if she closed her eyes tight and concentrated.

"It'll be a BIG responsibility," Lissa's mother said.

"I know — but what can we do?" Lissa's father said.

"It'll poo in the garden and dig up my flowers. It'll leave hairs on the furniture and wet tracks on the floor for me to clean up," Lissa's mother said.

But Lissa's father said, "We'll all do our share."

Lissa hugged herself she was so excited.

The next day Lissa was eating waffles and pretending she didn't
know anything about a dog, when her mother said. "Lissa, I've got
to talk to you about something important."

Lissa's mother sat down. "Listen," she said. "Your Granda and Grandma are moving out of their house and into a seniors' apartment. Your Grandma is having trouble with all the stairs in the house. Your Granda says he can't spend another winter shovelling snow. The new place will be great for them, but there's only one problem."

"Mmmm?" Lissa asked, her mouth full of waffle.

"Jingles," Lissa's mother said. "The dog. Jingles. Jingles can't go to the new apartment because dogs aren't allowed. And your grandparents won't move unless they're sure Jingles is taken care of. We've agreed to take Jingles to live with us. It'll be a BIG responsibility, but someone has to take him."

"Jingles!" Lissa said. She could hardly speak. Suddenly she didn't feel hungry anymore. Jingles was a big black dog with a foolish grin that showed all his teeth. He spent most of his time on the floor by the sofa, watching TV. He stole pizza and howled when piano music was played. Worst of all, Jingles wasn't a puppy. In dog-years, Lissa thought, Jingles must be as old as her grandparents!

Lissa ran out in the yard. "Well, I'M not having anything to do with him," she told a striped cat and two chickadees. "I want a puppy!" she shouted.

When Lissa and her parents went to help her grandparents move, they all helped carry furniture and pictures and boxes of glass dishes. Lissa dusted the picture frames and made angry faces at Jingles. Afterwards, everyone had pizza and Jingles stole the second helpings.

"Oh Jingles," Granda said softly, "how we'll miss you!" He told Lissa how Jingles had come into their lives. It had been around Christmas, and the plows had made snowbanks as high as the living room window. On one of those banks, a dog had stood and looked into the warm room. Night after night, he'd watched and stared until Granda and Grandma opened the door to him.

"He chose us," Grandma said. "Now we're choosing you. You'll love him."

Then Lissa and her parents took Jingles home.

Lissa's mother didn't have much experience with dogs in cars. She put Jingles in the back seat with Lissa, and made him sit up like a person so she could put a seat belt on him. Jingles grinned foolishly at Lissa, showing all his teeth. There were grey hairs in his black fur.

"He smells awful," Lissa said.

"He just needs a bath," said Lissa's father.

"YOU give him one," said Lissa.

With Jingles, things really changed at Lissa's house. A dog really was a BIG responsibility. Jingles cried if he was left alone for a long time. In the backyard, Jingles left most of the flowers alone, but he liked to eat mint and oregano. Jingles got really excited whenever a certain white cat appeared, and went crashing through the rosebushes after her. He left a trail of broken stems and crushed petals. And when the pizza delivery man arrived, Jingles stood on his hind legs and yelped and yowled at him and tried to bite the pizza box.

But there were good things about Jingles too. Lissa had to admit it.
In the park, when a big boy knocked Lissa off her bike, Jingles
bared his teeth and growled. The big boy got scared and ran off. At
Lissa's birthday party, Jingles got tangled up in streamers, and all
Lissa's friends laughed and said, "What a great dog! He's SO
funny!" Jingles let Lissa's friends pet him. And when Lissa was in
the living room building cities with her blocks, Jingles just lay on
the floor close to her, watching the cities grow and keeping Lissa
company.

Still, Lissa tried not to like Jingles too much. She didn't pet him very much. She still thought about the Dog-Next-Year she was supposed to get, just for herself. She thought of the puppy she wanted, of the long silky ears and brown and white fur. She thought of the puppy's secret name, and said it to herself so that she wouldn't forget it.

One Saturday it was finally warm enough to go to the beach. Lissa had been waiting for this day ever since her last snowman melted. She packed her buckets and sand molds and her special box for collecting treasures. At the beach, Lissa hurried over the big rocks, down to the water's edge where the sand was warm and as fine as sugar. She picked up a piece of driftwood and tossed it into the ocean. "Fetch, Jingles!" she shouted, but Jingles only followed the stick with his eyes, then hurried off to investigate tidal pools.

"Hi," a boy said. He was standing next to Lissa. "Is that your dog?"

"Sort of," Lissa said.

"Nice dog," the boy said. "I'd love to have a dog. You're lucky. I'm Sam. Can I play with him too?"

"Yeah, you can play with him," she said.

"What's his name?"

"Jingles," she said. "And I'm Lissa."

Jingles came running up the beach. He was wet and excited and carrying something small in his mouth. He was wagging his tail hard, and sprinkling water drops on everyone he passed.

"Git out of here, dog!" someone shouted. "You got me soaked."

Jingles dropped the small thing at Lissa's feet. It was a starfish, perfectly shaped, pale purple and dried by the sun.

"He brought you a present," Sam said.

"I guess he did," said Lissa.

Jingles looked like he was waiting for something, a thank-you, perhaps. Lissa took the starfish. She ran her hands over its spiny hardness, then put it in her special box. Then she leaned over and put her arms around Jingles, really hugged him hard for the first time.

Jingles smelled of sand, sun, the salty wet insides of tidal pools—
and himself. His ears were soft and silky. And, underneath, where
it wasn't wet, his old black fur was softer and warmer than Lissa
could have ever imagined. Lissa felt something warming her
inside the way the sun was warming her outside. It felt awfully
good.

Lissa stood up. "C'mon, Jingles," she said, "you old pirate. Come help Sam and me find some more treasures." She raced down the beach.

Her dog ran after her.